Have fun learning how to count, color, and create!

Graphic design: Karen Bowlding
Illustrations by: Crystal Middleton

ISBN: 978-0-578-87947-5

Printed in the United States 2021

Dedication

This book is dedicated to all the children I've enjoyed creating with throughout the years.

Ten Messy Fingers

Ten messy fingers on my face

Ten messy fingers all over the place

On my paper, on my clothes

In my hair and on my toes

Tub time is near

Ten messy fingers will soon disappear

1

One white rectangle.

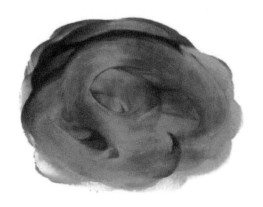

2

Two green blotches.

3

Three blue clouds.

4

Four yellow hearts.

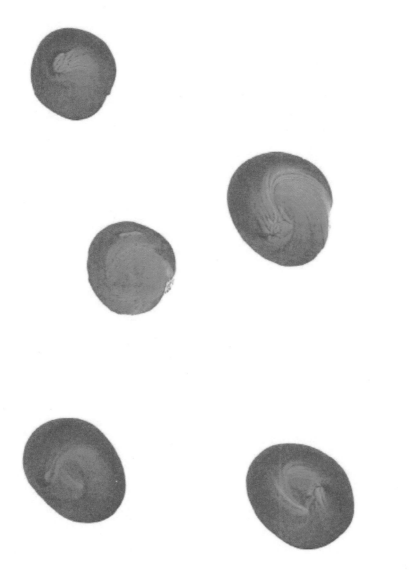

5

Five red circles.

6

Six purple triangles.

7

Seven brown squares.

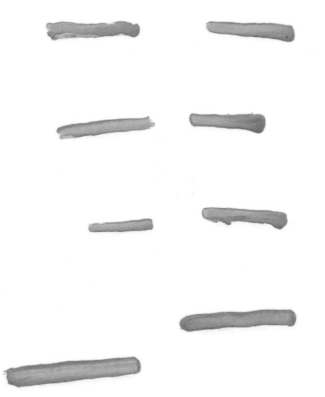

8

Eight orange lines.

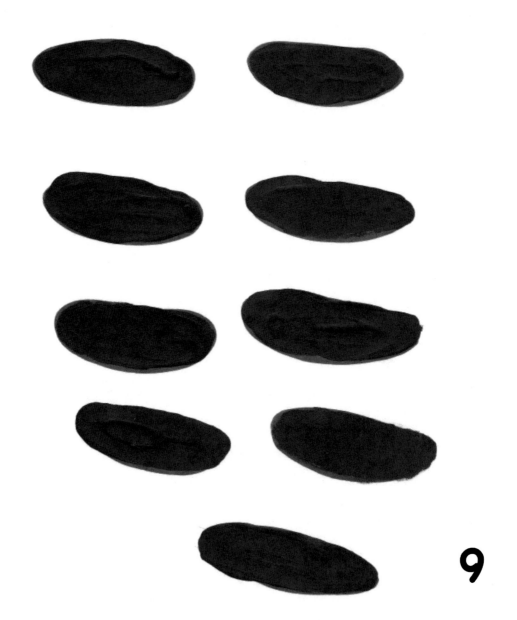

9

Nine black ovals.

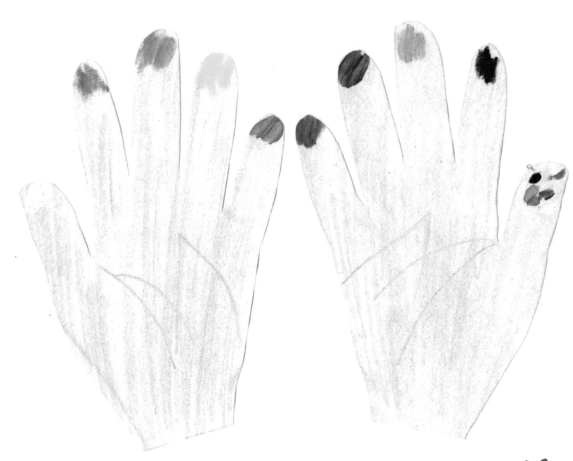

10

Ten messy fingers.

Which numbers do you know?

1 2 3 4 5
6 7 8 9 10

Which colors do you know?

Red White Blue

Orange Black Yellow

Green Purple

How many shapes do you know?

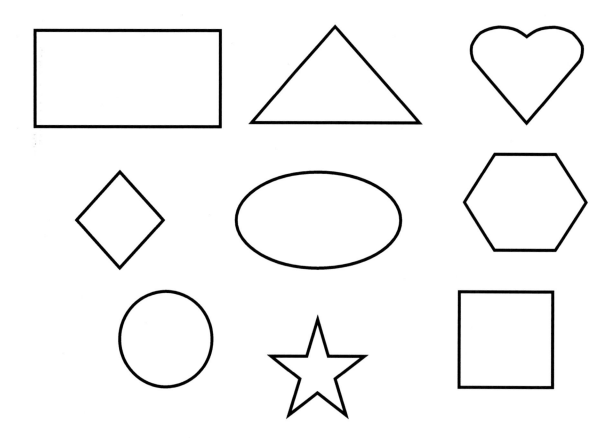

This book belongs to:

_____

Trace your hands.

Note to Parents

Children love to learn, use this book to teach or revisit knowledge of shapes, numbers and colors. Encourage your child to have fun and be creative.

About the Author

Crystal Middleton is married and a mother of three boys. She has worked in the public school system for over 15 years. The oldest of 10 children, she has always enjoyed working with young children. Creating art projects and seeing the smile on a child's face after they have learned something new brings her joy.

Contact

crys.r.middleton@gmail.com

Made in the USA
Middletown, DE
08 April 2021